Aesop's F

retold by Geraldine McCaughrean

Contents

Introduction	2
The Hare and the Tortoise	4
Borrowed Plumes	10
Wolf! Wolf!	14
Ant and Grasshopper	20
Get Well Soon	24
Woolly Wolf	27
Thin In, Stout Out	32
King Frog	34
Wind and Sun	40
A Dog's Life	46

Introduction

Fables are stories with a message. There is a lesson to be learned from them. But Aesop's Fables won't teach you how to be a kind, good person. They say more about how to survive, how to avoid the pitfalls other fools fall into.

If you believe Aesop, the world is full of tricksters, snobs, unkind friends, jealous neighbours, lying villains and idiots. Even though many of his characters are animals, Aesop was not writing about the way that animals behave. He was talking about you, me and everyone else.

If he ever existed at all (and some people doubt it), Aesop lived about 2500 years ago in Greece. Some of his stories existed before then – one was painted on a Pharaoh's papyrus scroll – so perhaps Aesop only collected fables. Legend says that Aesop was hurled to his death off a cliff, so he might have been right, after all, about the nastiness of human nature!

Fables are stories with a message.

The Hare and the Tortoise

Speedy Hare thought she was faster than anything on four legs. She jeered and sneered at Slocum Tortoise. "You're so slow you make the lampposts look reckless! If we raced, I could finish, marry and have seven children before you passed half way!"

"Try me," said Slocum.

So a route was chosen for the race, a start line and a finishing post. Away went Speedy; her dust made the tortoise cough. Over the hill she pelted, stopping only to sign autographs. Looking back, she saw no sign of Slocum. "What a loser! Huh!"

The sun was warm. The roadside grass tasted sweet. Speedy curled up under a tree and dozed, chuckling to herself. "Fancy thinking he could beat me! I shall be up from here and home in three bounds!"

"Tumti-tumti-tum," hummed Slocum, plodding along the road. An ant overtook him, carrying a big grain of wheat. "Rumti-tumti-tum," hummed Slocum, plodding over the crest of the hill. "Rooti-toot."

Plod, plod, plod. His awkward, tubular legs trundled on. Through the wood, quietly, quietly past the sleeping hare. It took all day, but Slocum reached the finishing post.

"Where's Speedy?" asked the judge, presenting Slocum with a laurel wreath. At that very moment — ears flying, feet thumping, fast as a speeding bullet — the hare hurtled over the finish line: "I-win-I-win-I-win!!"

I-win-I-win-I-win!!

But she did not. She had not. Slocum was already being carried shoulder-high across the meadow. They called him "Lightning" after that. But the names they thought up for that silly hare I won't repeat.

Slow and steady wins the race.

Borrowed Plumes

A jackdaw, ambitious for better things, saw peacocks strutting on a manor house lawn. "Ah, now there is style! There is grandeur!" He picked up all the single feathers which fell from the peacocks' magnificent tails and soon had enough to make a tail for himself — a big, fanning tail of iridescent blues and greens.

"I am going to live among kindred spirits!" he declared to his fellow jackdaws. "I am moving up to better things!"

Of course his body did not quite match up to his tail. When the peacocks saw him, they sharpened their green beaks.

"Impudent impersonator!" Peck peck.

"Jackie jackanapes!" Peck peck.

"Jumped-up little jackdaw!" Peck peck.

With all his borrowed feathers gone, his ambition in tatters, Jackie Jackdaw hopped home.

But his fellow jackdaws were not glad to see him. Far from it.

"Thought you were too good for us, didn't you?" Peck peck.

"Gave yourself airs and graces, didn't you?" Peck peck.

"We thought we had seen the back of you!" Peck peck.

So he flew a long and lonely way away, and lived on his lonesome own, all sad and sorry – and really rather bald.

Don't try to be
something Nature
didn't make you.

Wolf! Wolf!

Tending sheep was a little too dull for Tom's liking. Nothing exciting happened from morning till night. So to add excitement, Tom came up with a game.

He stood on a tree-stump, cupped his hands round his mouth and yelled, as loud as he could: "HELP! WOLF!"

Of course, all the other shepherds came running, with pitchforks and guns and shepherds' crooks. "Where? Hold on boy! We're coming! We'll save you!"

Tom laughed so loud he frightened the sheep. "Tricked you!" he chanted as they spilled into sight scattering the flock. "Tricked you! Tricked you!" The shepherds wiped their sweaty brows and told him roundly never to do it again.

15

But Tom liked doing it. He did it time after time: up on the tree-stump, hands cupped round his mouth: "WOOOLF! HELP!!!"

Everyone came running. What a laugh! Tee-hee-hee.

Then one day, while Tom was dozing, he felt a wet nose in his ear, a shaggy paw on his knee. He looked the wolf in its yellow eyes and the wolf looked back, letting a red tongue loll out over its sharp yellow teeth.

Tom yelled. Oh yes, he yelled louder than he had ever yelled in his life before. "W-W-W-W-WOOOOLF!" and then again!!!! "W-W-W-W-WOOOOLF!"

But nobody came. They assumed it was only Tom being silly again, playing that tired old trick on them. And they were sick of tricks.

So they did not miss him till bedtime. And by then, of course, it was much, much too late.

No one believes a liar, even when he's telling the truth.

Ant and Grasshopper

Summer. The Grasshopper played the cello with her back legs, and basked in the warmth. "What you a-doing, Ant," she asked, "always bustling about?"

"Busy, busy, busy," said the Ant racing past with a grain of wheat. "Preparing for winter. So should you."

"Later, later," groaned the
Grasshopper. "Who wants to think
about winter in the summertime?"
And her antennae waved in time
to her music.

Winter. The grass was pin-stiff with frost, but deep below it the Ant rested cosy in his nest. The shelves were lined with food, so were the cellars and lofts. A live-in larder.

Someone came knocking at the Ant's door. "Oh, spare me a bite to eat, neighbour!" wailed the Grasshopper, thin as wire, legs all out of tune.

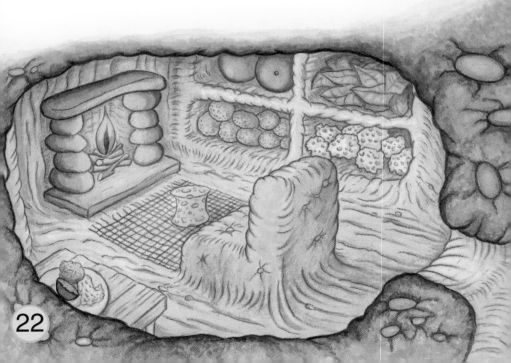

"You should have thought of that in the summer!" shouted the Ant through his letterbox. "I warned you. Now you must pay for your gallivanting!" And back he went, to sit out winter in his great, silent larder.

Thrift and hard work: the secret of success!

Get Well Soon

Word went out that Lion was ill – very ill – dying.

"Before he dies, the King wishes to say goodbye to his loyal subjects!" brayed his heralds, the hyenas. "In his cave."

So the animals put on sad faces and trotted off to Lion's den. All day they visited, one by one, carrying flowers in their teeth. By sundown only Fox had not visited.

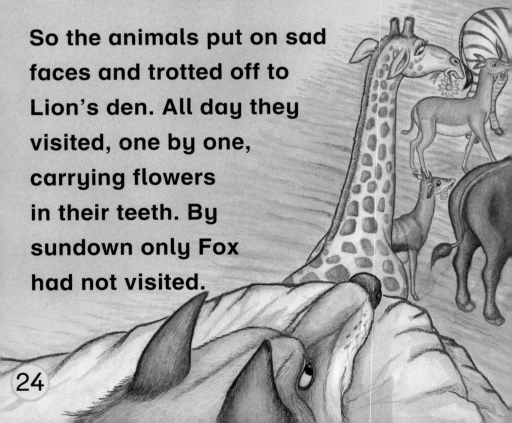

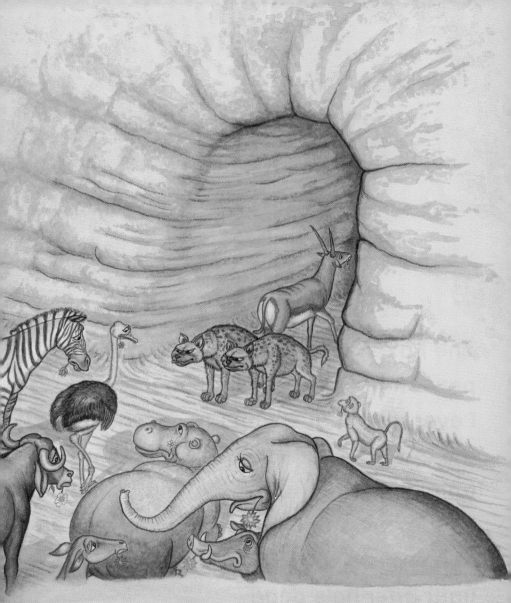

"Shame on you, Fox!" said the King's herals. "Show some respect to your King!"

The Fox swished his red tail. "Oh paw-on-heart, I respect him as much as I ever did. That's why I have watched the cave door all day. I have seen animals going in, but I haven't seen a single one come out again. So, with all due respect to His Majesty, I'll wait until *after* he's dead before I go in there and wish him well."

Keep your wits about you. It's a jungle out there.

Woolly Wolf

Wolfie thought up a terrific ruse for catching his supper. He knitted himself a woollen coat and bleated outside the sheepfold until he was let in. His sheep disguise fooled the sheep completely, and whenever he was hungry, all he had to do was unbutton his sheep suit, poke out his nose and – snap! Lamb for lunch, dinner and tea.

The shepherd saw that his flock was dwindling, checked the fences, found no gaps where a wolf might get in. Shepherds, though, have rather more brains than sheep.

Meanwhile, Wolfie grew greedy. He ate snacks between his meals. He ate snacks between his snacks. So his woollen coat was often unbuttoned. Lamb for elevenses, lamb niblets.

"I see your game! shouted a voice behind him. "Wait till I get hold of you!"

Over the fence went Wolfie, but the shepherd was hard on his woolly heels. *Wham!* went the shepherd's crook. *Wham! Blam!* on Woolfie's woolly back.

"John, John!" called the other shepherds. "Is that any way to round up sheep?"

"This is no sheep!" called John in reply. "It's a wolf in sheep's clothing, and when I catch him, so help me, he'll know how it feels to be roast lamb!"

Every cheat gets found out in the end.

Thin In, Stout Out

A hungry mouse found a tiny hole in a basket of grain. In she went, like a thread through a needle's eye, thin and quick and sharp with hunger. Inside, she found Mouse Heaven, wall-to-wall food, grain more than she thought she could eat.

But she ate it.

When it came to getting out, the hole was the same size, but the mouse was bigger. Much bigger. Wall-to-wall mouse, in fact.

"Help!" she complained. "Help! Help!"

"Don't worry," said a passing weasel. "You'll get out."

"When? When?" wailed the voice inside the basket.

"When you're as thin as when you went in," said the weasel.

When will I get out?

When you're as thin as when you went in.

Greedyguts.

King Frog

Peace dappled the pond with birdsong
and dragonflies. The frogs sat about
with nothing to do but eat, think and
blink their bulbous eyes.

"Dull, dull, dull," agreed the frogs.

"What we need is a king," said one. So they prayed to the gods, and Jupiter (with a twitch of a smile) dropped a log into the pool: SPLOOSH! King Log.

What a stir that made! All the frogs jumped higher than Olympic pole vaulters. Then the ripples spread and died. The log lay lolling, log-like in the pond, and the frogs all blew bubbles of awe.

After a year or two in this peaceful kingdom, the frogs said, "Boring, boring, boring. We need the kind of king who will make a difference!" And they glooped so many froggy prayers at Heaven that Jupiter could barely hear himself think.

"A new king?" he said, frowning.
"Very well." And he sent down a stork.
A legs-like-reeds, feet-like-crabs, beak-like-a-rapier, hunger-like-a-wolf sort of stork, who ate and ate and ate. When he had finished eating, he flew away, to look for more food.

Peace mottled the pond with falling leaves and lily pads. Nothing disturbed the soothing lap-lap of the water — not one bulbous eye blinking, not so much as a croak. For the stork had eaten every frog.

Some people
don't realise when
they are well off!

39

Wind and Sun

Sun and Wind quarrelled one day.
"I'm best!" bawled bully Wind.
"I'm strongest!"

"Want to bet?" the Sun said softly.
She nodded her orange curls in the
direction of a man walking far below.
"For example, could you strip
him stitchless?"

Wind brayed loudly. "Ha! Nothing to it.
I'll blow him bare!" And he began to
blow. Away went the man's hat. His
coat flapped. The money in his
pockets jingled. But he only pulled
his coat tighter round him and
fastened the buttons.

Wind blew still harder, tipping tiles off roofs, lifting litter. But the man only buckled his belt and turned up his collar.

Wind blew till trees fell over and sheep bowled downhill. But the man only ducked his head and struggled into the shelter of his house.

Wind blew himself blue, then he wheezed, "Well? Can you do any better?"

Sun shone. The man came out of doors and looked at the sky. "What strange weather we're having!" he said.

Sun shone. The man took off his gloves and scarf.

Sun shone and shone. The man unbuttoned his coat, took it off, loosened his collar, wiped his brow.

Sun shone. With a quick glance round, the man turned on his garden hose and danced naked under the spray. "Lovely, lovely weather we're having!" he sang.

Sun said nothing. She did not have to. Wind had already stormed away into a far corner of the sky, where he stayed and sulked for a month.

Brute force is not
the best way to win
friends and influence
people.

45

A Dog's Life

A wolf and a dog got talking. At least, the dog talked.

"Two meals a day, a bed by the fire, strokes and pats and titbits off the table! And all I have to do in return is chase sticks and rabbits and bark at burglars. Oh yes, my life is pretty much perfect!"

The wolf was envious, no question about it. "I only have to look at you to see it is true. Your coat is glossy, your eyes are bright ... But tell me, what is that line round your neck where the fur is worn thin?"

"Oh that." The dog shrugged. "That's only where my collar chafes when they chain me up at night."

The wolf blinked his yellow eyes and trotted farther off. "I was going to ask if I could come and serve your master. But I just changed my mind."

Freedom is better than the most luxurious prison.